# That's a Good One!

# That's a Good One!

## A Collection of Jokes

## Philip Reiss

*Illustrated by Sami Reiss*

**VANTAGE PRESS**
New York

FIRST EDITION

All rights reserved, including the right of
reproduction in whole or in part in any form.

Copyright © 1998 by Philip Reiss

Published by Vantage Press, Inc.
516 West 34th Street, New York, New York 10001

Manufactured in the United States of America
ISBN: 0-533-12429-8

Library of Congress Catalog Card No.: 97-90579

0 9 8 7 6 5 4 3 2 1

For Sarah Lewin, Sami and Maya Reiss, Jennie and Samuel Coskey, and in memory of Isaac Reiss and Samuel Reiss

# Foreword

Our late uncle, the author, composed these jokes over a period of years. He collected and organized them before his death in 1995. We would like to thank all who helped in the making of this book, in particular his sister, Sarah Lewin.

—Levi and Noga Reiss
—Judy and Ted Coskey

# That's a Good One!

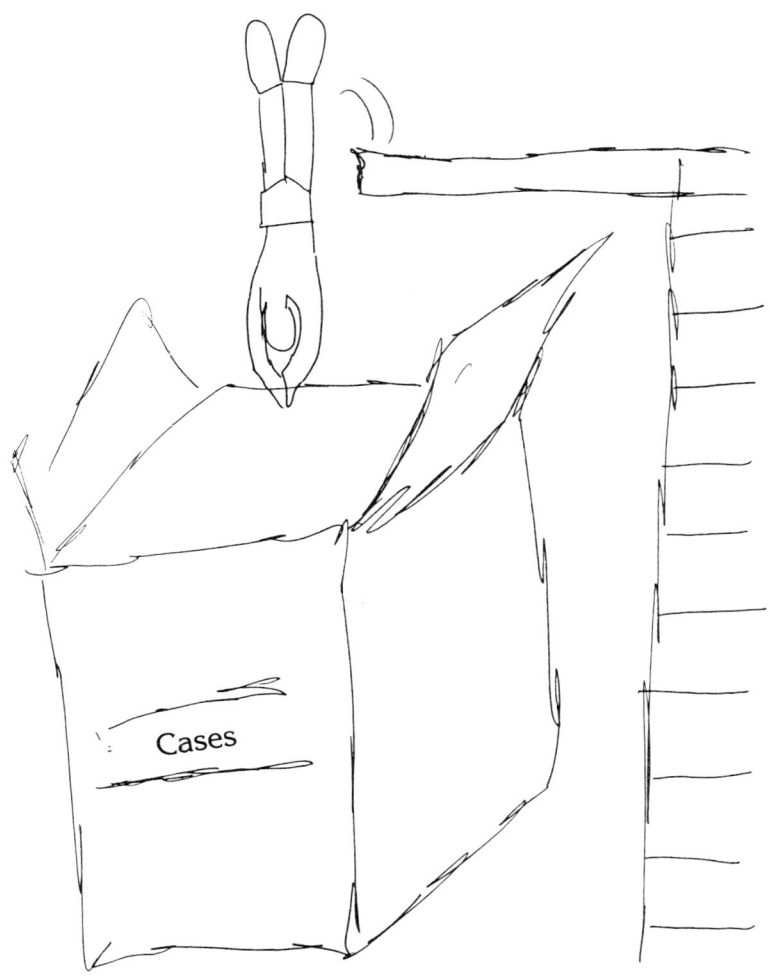

Chief of Detectives—Fanny, I've got a tough case for you.

Detective—Now, Chief, why must you always call me Fanny?

Chief—Because you get to the bottom so fast.

A bully married a woman who wouldn't back down on her rights and often led with a left.

*   *   *

Mabel—Years ago when it cost three cents to mail a letter, I used to lick the stamp! Today, at thirty-two cents, I spit on it!

Judge—Didn't your father teach you the road to success was honesty?
Defendant—Yes, Your Honor, but I have such a poor sense of direction.

Wife—How dare they. Sending us pornographic pictures in the mail! Do something!

Husband—Yes, dear, I'll look into it immediately.

A lively old-timer made a pass at a young woman and was rewarded with a cold stare.
Old-Timer—Oh, come on! I'm not so old! Why, I was born in nineteen-forty!
Young Woman—Is that so! A.D. or B.C.?

Piano Teacher—Are you keeping up with your lessons at home?
Student—Yes, sir. I can now play Chopin's Minute Waltz in less than an hour!

\*   \*   \*

Dad—What are you studying in college now?
Son—I'll find out at the end of the semester!

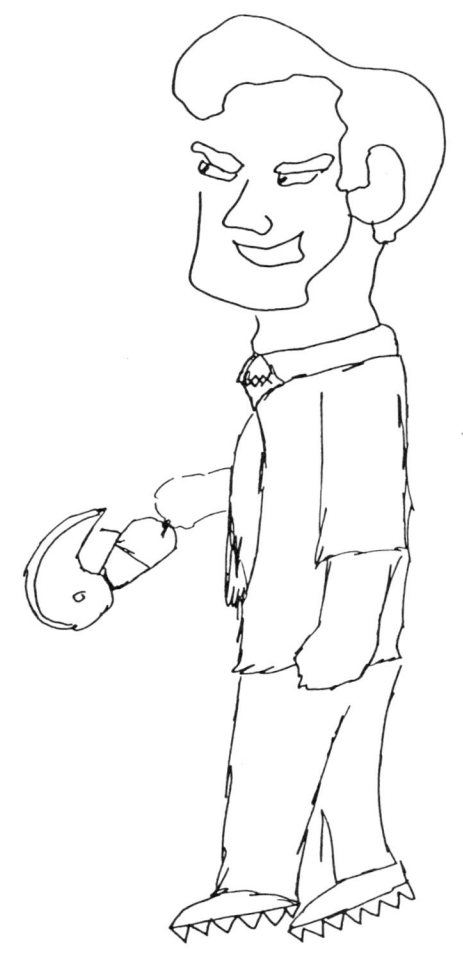

Gail [taking off her shoe and rubbing her toes]—Clayton, you may be a smooth politician, but as a dancer, you have two left feet.

Clayton—Hush, Gail! Two right feet perhaps; remember this is a conservative party dance.

Eve—You've been cold to me lately. Are you looking for another woman?
Adam—No! You know I love only one woman.

\* \* \*

On a New Year's day celebration, you'll know the New Year has come in when your guests have passed out.

Man's determination to break the sound barrier began when a scientist tried to get a word in, once his wife started to talk.

* * *

Dudley—We've been living together for seven years and always managed to settle our quarrels peacefully. What do you say we get married?
Etta—What! And give you grounds for divorce!

Professor Andre—My American wife, Alba, wants me to teach her French.

Professor Henri—After years of marriage, I suppose she's finally decided to order a dinner in French herself, and not have to rely on you.

Professor Andre—No, it isn't that. She told me she's called me every name she knows in English.

Bill—Pay me the money you owe me!
Gill—You'll get it. I'm short.
Bill—I want it now. I can't wait till you grow up.

*   *   *

Husband—What do you suggest to improve my wife's appearance?
Magician [after quick appraisal]—Her disappearance.

A husband was about to chop off the head of the Thanksgiving turkey when his wife interrupted.
Wife—That's cruel. Isn't there some other way?
Husband—Well, I might give the turkey one of those "looks that kill" you sometimes give me.

A playwright sent his play to a producer. The producer read it, and returned it with the following advice.
Producer—Your play has a beginning, a middle, but no end. I strongly recommend you make an end to it.

\* \* \*

With medical expenses so high, women are having their babies delivered by the postman.

Polly—How are you making out with your reducing diet?

Molly—Fine! I'm gaining weight much slower!

Fran—So! What do you do when your husband barks at you like a dog?
Sybil—I don't mind.
Fran—You don't get angry?
Sybil—No.
Fran—Why?
Sybil—Because he's barking at me like a dog, man's best friend.

Chubby—I don't depend on nutritionists to tell me what to eat. A skillful waiter will always bring you a balanced meal.

Slim—I'd like to buy your horse.
Tim—You can have him for a thousand.
Slim—I'll give you one hundred for both.
Tim—There ain't but one animal here.
Slim—I see two! If you think I'll give you a thousand dollars for old swayback, you must be a jackass.

Dad—How are you doing with your studies in college?
Son—Great, I don't start studying till the professor throws the book at me!

\* \* \*

Judge—Haven't I seen you before?
Thief—Yes, Your Honor. You treated me fair the last time, so I'm giving you repeat business.

The minister urged his congregation always to look up for help.

Confused member—Now I don't know what to do! Last Sunday I found ten dollars on the sidewalk.

Barry—Why did you divorce your wife? You told me your relationship was one hundred percent.
Marvin—Yeh, I gave her one hundred percent love! She gave me one hundred percent hate!

"Look at me," said the embezzler, depressed. "I had my clothes made to order; now I wear a prison uniform."

"Look at me," said the pickpocket proudly. "I was always dressed in rags; now my clothes are made to order!"

Daisy—I heard you stopped seeing Archie.
Shirley—No, I'm seeing him more often. I'm trying hard to convince him we're through.

*   *   *

Teacher—Alvin, tell me the meaning of the sentence I just said.
Student—[Mumbling] It was . . .
Teacher—I can't make out what you're saying.
Student—Would you like me to repeat myself?
Teacher—No, thank you. One of you is enough.

A mechanic advised his daughter, make a bolt if a nut makes a grab for you!

Apartment seeker—I'm looking for an apartment.
Landlord—I rent my apartments only to tenants who don't quarrel.
Apartment seeker—No problem! My wife and I stopped talking to each other years ago.

\* \* \*

Judge—On what grounds do you want a divorce?
Geologist—On any grounds! As long as they're not quicksand.

Grandson—I hate the thought of getting old.
Grandpa—Oh! 'Taint so bad. That's the time you forget all the mistakes you made when you were young!

* * *

Music student—Do you think I'll ever be a finished musician?
Music teacher—You already are!

Prize fighter—When I hit you, you'll know who hit you!
Opponent—And when I hit you, you *won't* know who hit you!

\*   \*   \*

Wife—I have nothing to wear to the masquerade ball!
Husband—Good! Everyone will see you have nothing to hide!

Egbert—I'd like to marry you again!
Della—But I divorced you for incompatibility.
Egbert—It took five years for you to discover all my faults. Since then I've acquired enough new faults to last us another five.

Herbert—Congratulate me. I married Aileen.

Fanny—What? You married Aileen? She's been on the shelf for years!

Herbert—Yeh! I know! But she's so well preserved.

Moe—I don't feel so good lately.
Joe—I know what's wrong with you!
Moe—You do? Tell me!
Joe—It's your lifestyle! All you do is eat and sleep. Eat and sleep! Eat and sleep!
Moe—You're right! From now on I'll only eat and eat, eat and eat, eat and eat!

Lila [with a sneer at her new boyfriend]—You don't smoke! You don't drink! What else don't you do?

* * *

Wife—Your dentist gave you a great set of choppers. That steak disappeared in no time.
Husband—Yeh! Now take a look at the bill.
Wife—Wow! He took a big bite out of you!

Jeb—I'm so absent-minded! I would forget my name! But Tom is such an easy name to remember!

* * *

Jake—Is Henrietta giving you the divorce?
Ben—No! She decided we're a perfect mismatch.

Sig—I always found Greek easy.
Gus—You're joking!
Sig—No! Everything I ever studied was Greek to me.

\* \* \*

Psychiatrist—What lead you to drink?
Jasper—My wife Katrina. She's an intoxicating woman!

Ezra—Come on, Zeak, brighten up! Be your old self!

Zeak—I am my old self! I wanna be my young self.

A hangin' judge out West considered himself lenient. He handed out only suspended sentences.

*   *   *

Sergeant [shouting]—Pendleton! What the hell is wrong with you? Everybody's passed the parachute test except for you.
Pendleton—Well, Sarge, I had to land on a tree. The sign said keep off the grass.

The world is so immoral even a dog has a mistress.

\*   \*   \*

Drunken driver—Whoa, there! No more high octane for you!

\*   \*   \*

Jed the janitor decided he had enough dirt to change his profession to writer. All the critics acclaimed him, saying he had great sweep.

Gang Leader—Son! I don't want to hear any more! You're taking over the gang! I'm too old.

Son—But, Pa! I wanna be a doctor. There's more money in medicine!

Music student [removing music sheet]—I would like to play without music.
Music teacher—You've been doing it all the time.

        \*   \*   \*

Jason—I sometimes get the feeling you don't really love me!
Ella—And sometimes I get the feeling I really love you.

Judging by the size of their bellies, some old people are not nearly as concerned with their past, as with repast.

* * *

Old man Mose—I had hard luck all my life!
Old man Casper—You can't complain. You might have died young and had no luck at all!

There's a crying need for laughter.

* * *

Beethoven finished the fifth so he could finish
   the fourth.

* * *

Heckler [to comedian]—I didn't understand your last joke.
Comedian—Buddy, don't worry about it. I don't understand it either.

Music Student—I should have won the contest! My execution was the best!
Music Judge—Well! I voted for your execution.

* * *

Jack—We both married WACs, how come your WAC looks so young and mine so old?
Bertrand—My WAC was in camouflage.

Wife—Did you ask the boss for a raise?
Husband—Yes.
Wife—Did you get it?
Husband—No.
Wife—Why?
Husband—He said I have great drive, but in the wrong direction.

Prize fighter—I don't want to hurt my opponent. I only want to make a good impression.

Ellen—How am I doin', Doc?
Doctor—Get ready to die. I gave you the best medicine and your body refused it!
Ellen—I heard laughter was the best medicine. Tell me a joke.

\*   \*   \*

Teacher—Answer my question!
Student—I don't remember! I have two different ears! The question went in one ear and out the other!

Lester—It can't be true!
Hubert—What can't be true?
Lester—That the Indian population grows by the millions every year!
Hubert—What's so surprising about that?
Lester—How! With so many untouchables!

Chauvinist—Do you approve of clubs for men only?
Feminist—Yes, on the head!

* * *

Young woman—Doctor, help me. I can't stand the size of my rear end!
Doctor [viewing her behind]—You must get control of yourself. Eating your heart out won't reduce your bottom.

He's so dishonest, even if he swore he's a thief, you couldn't believe him.

\*   \*   \*

Composer—How did you like my new composition?
Critic—I didn't care for its beginning or the middle, but I enjoyed its ending.

Wife—What are you doing home so early?
Husband—I was fired.
Wife—You told me the boss said you fired him with enthusiasm.
Husband—No! I said *he* fired *me* with enthusiasm.

\* \* \*

"I don't go for a pick-me-up," said the boozer. "When I feel low, I switch from suspenders to a belt."

Census taker—Sir, how old are you?

Old-timer—I don't remember. I was born so long ago.

Edgar [the boss delivering his holiday talk]—Men! When I was working for a living, all I ever got for a bonus was food for thought!

\*   \*   \*

Dina—On our honeymoon you called me sugarplum. Now you call me sugar bowl.

Warden [to forger]—Why is it you can copy everyone's signature but you sign your own name with an X?
Forger—My pa told me, son, you have talent! No use wastin' time on education.

      \*   \*   \*

Humorist [to audience]—I wasn't always a wit. Like any other craft, it takes time to develop. I started out as a half-wit.

Harold—I got my money the hard way.
Mike—Come on! A rich guy like you! You never did a day's work in your life!
Harold—Not me! My father.

It was Grandpa's hundredth birthday and he was given a big party. Reporters crowded him to tell the secret of his long life.

Grandpa—Fruits and vegetables!

Reporters—Fruits and vegetables?

Grandpa—Yep! Never touched 'em!

Felix—I heard you have a great relationship with your wife. What's your secret?
Hank—No secret! We share everything fifty-fifty, love and hate.

Prize fighter—You're so dumb! You can't even write your name!
Opponent—[Punches him in the eye] You're right! All I ever learned was to dot the eyes!